Smudger the Dog Saves ~~Ru~~ Christmas

SAVES

by Lissa Evans illustrated by Holly Surplice

RED FOX

It was a puzzling sort of evening.

For some reason, people kept hiding from Smudger.

The kitchen was full of unusual and interesting smells.

There were socks
hanging at just
the right height.

And there was a small
tree in the house.

Smudger went out for a breath of fresh air.

He did a little work
in the garden.

And a little more.

And while he was busy . . .
some visitors arrived.

Smudger loved having visitors.
He went to greet them.

And then . . .

and then . . .

Smudger hated having to wait for anything.
It made him anxious.

So he had a light,
leathery snack

to soothe his nerves.

And then, at last,
it was time to go.

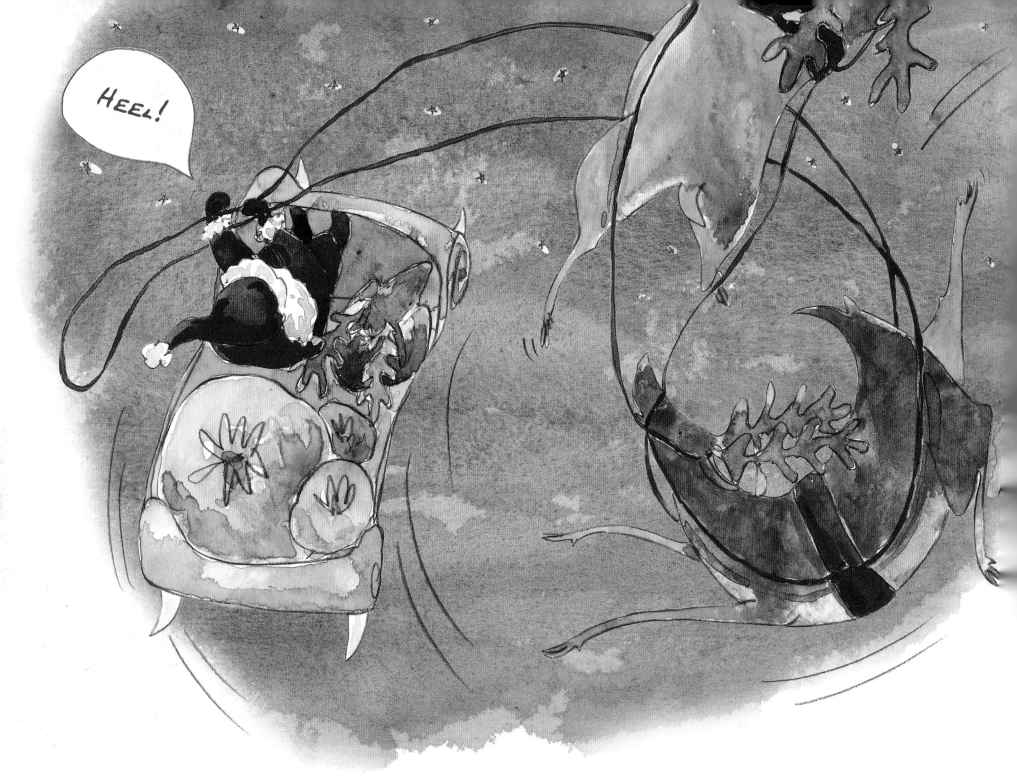

Smudger hadn't been expecting a night-time walk, so he was quite excited.
He ran in a couple of circles . . .

HEEL! HEEL!

and woofed once
        or twice,

before checking out
        a delicious smell or two.

SMUDGER!

And then . . .

Smudger felt dreadfully ashamed,

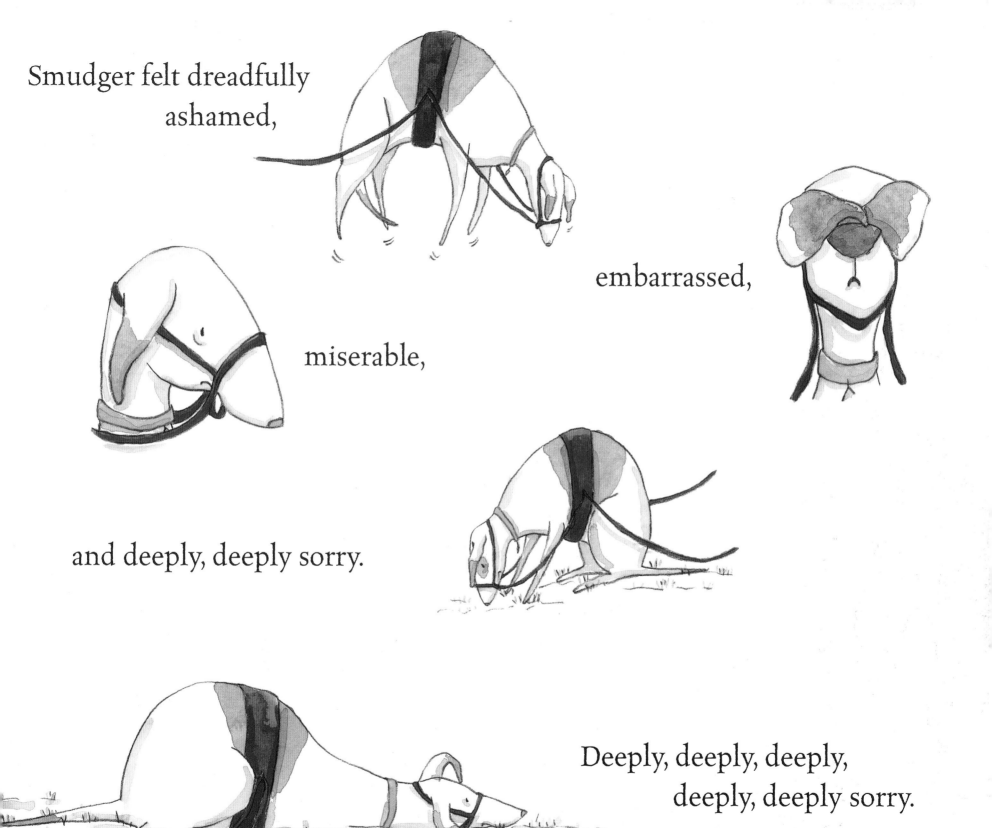

embarrassed,

miserable,

and deeply, deeply sorry.

Deeply, deeply, deeply, deeply, deeply sorry.

And then it was time
for ANOTHER walk!

And it was wonderful.

Smudger had never known that there
were so many beautiful smells
in the world.

The wonderful walk went
on and on,

and on
and on,

and on
and on
and on.

And somewhere in the middle of the night, in the middle of the fog,
in the middle of nowhere . . .

Smudger started to think about how nice it would be
to get back to his own warm house,

where there were
cushions to lie on and
people who wanted
to stroke his ears.

And he started to sniff the air.

And he sniffed and he sniffed
until suddenly . . .

... he caught a tiny whiff of home.
But it was in the other direction.

He had to
do something
quickly.

Smudger ran faster than he had ever run before.

And when he got home . . .

OH, THERE YOU ARE. I WAS JUST STARTING TO GET WORRIED.

. . . the back door was open

and somebody wanted to stroke his ears.

He was very tired, but before he went to bed
he inspected the kitchen,
just to make sure that everything
had been put away properly.

And then he checked
out the socks again,

before going to see if the small
tree was still in the house.

The next morning,
Smudger woke early.

MUM, NONE OF THE LIGHTS ARE WORKING.

ALL THE MINCE PIES HAVE BEEN EATEN!

He had a good stretch

. . . . COMPLETELY RUINED EVERYTHING!

and then he went out
into the garden.

He knew he was happy.
What he didn't know was that he had
(single-handedly) saved Christmas.

To Badger, the dog who's saved many Christmases – LE
For Honey, with lots of Christmas kisses from Mummy xxx – HS

SMUDGER THE DOG SAVES CHRISTMAS
A RED FOX BOOK 978 1 862 30979 1

First published in Great Britain by Red Fox,
an imprint of Random House Children's Books
A Random House Group Company

This edition published 2010

1 3 5 7 9 10 8 6 4 2

Text copyright © Lissa Evans, 2010
Illustrations copyright © Holly Surplice, 2010

Red Fox Books are published by Random House Children's Books,
61–63 Uxbridge Road, London W5 5SA

www.kidsatrandomhouse.co.uk
www.rbooks.co.uk

Addresses for companies within The Random House Group Limited can be found at: www.randomhouse.co.uk/offices.htm

THE RANDOM HOUSE GROUP Limited Reg. No. 954009

A CIP catalogue record for this book is available from the British Library.

Printed in China